For Benjamin Wilder

Library of Congress Cataloging-in-Publication Data available.

ISBN 978-1-4521-8436-4

Manufactured in China.

Design by Lydia Ortiz and Abbie Goveia.
Typeset in Zemke Hand.

10 9 8 7 6 5 4 3 2 1

Chronicle Books LLC
680 Second Street
San Francisco, California 94107

Chronicle Books—we see things differently.
Become part of our community at www.chroniclekids.com.

My CHRISTMAS WISH for YOU

Lisa Swerling & Ralph Lazar

chronicle books · san francisco

Each star you see on Christmas Eve . . .

is a wish that's come true
for those who believe.

So many millions
of wishes come true!

Here are a handful
that I wish for you . . .

Christmas tree baubles,
gold angels and bells,

holly on doorways,
and wonderful smells.

Colorful ribbons
with gifts in a row,

stockings by chimneys,
and fires aglow.

Snowflakes that settle
on wonderlands white,

cheeks flushed and rosy,
eyes glistening bright.

Candlelit windows
and magical homes,

dazzling Santas,
striped candy, and gnomes.

Mittens and snowballs,

snow angels and boots,

snowmen and sledding
with hollers and hoots.

Mugs of hot chocolate
for tummies' delight,

breathing like dragons

to warm up the night.

Friends joined together
in goodwill and song,

a welcome to others...
the sense you belong.

The glimpse of a sleigh
and a tinkling bell . . .

A red nose! A reindeer!
A beard we know well.

The hope that this Christmas
Saint Nick with his sack

will stop at your chimney
and slide down the stack.

Snuggles and cuddles
and loved ones to hold,

eyelids grown heavy
as stories are told.

Memories and moments,
wide smiles and eyes,

surprises to treasure,
no matter the size.

I wish you the joy
of giving, as well . . .

a poem
or promise,

a feather
or shell.

I wish heaps of good cheer
through all of the land,

and the brightest of stars
to be held in your hand.

So it's always in reach
and you always will know,

you carry it with you

wherever you go.

Wherever you travel, whatever you do,

and not just on Christmas

but EVERY day, too!